Blue Bug tried to

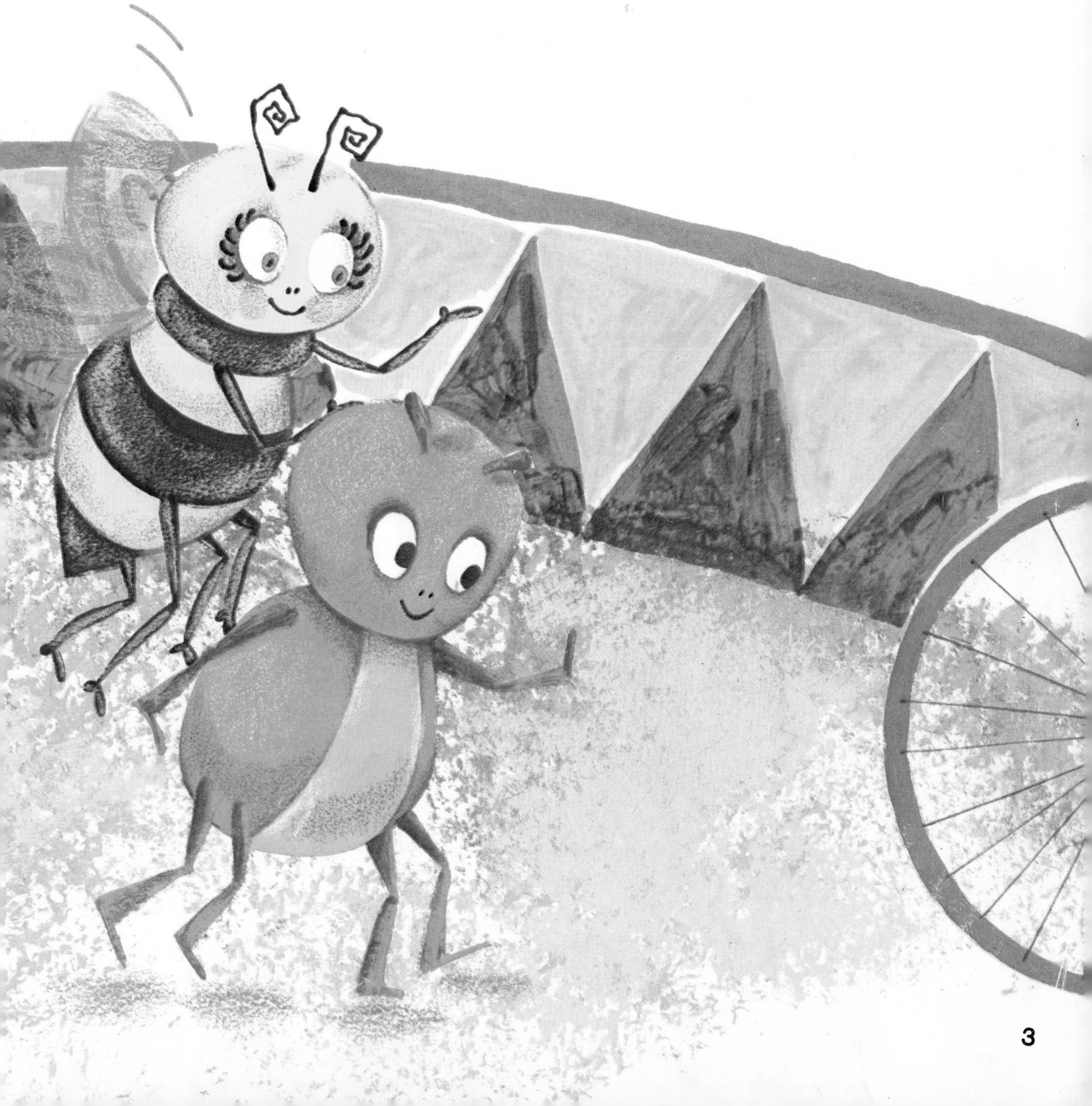

ride

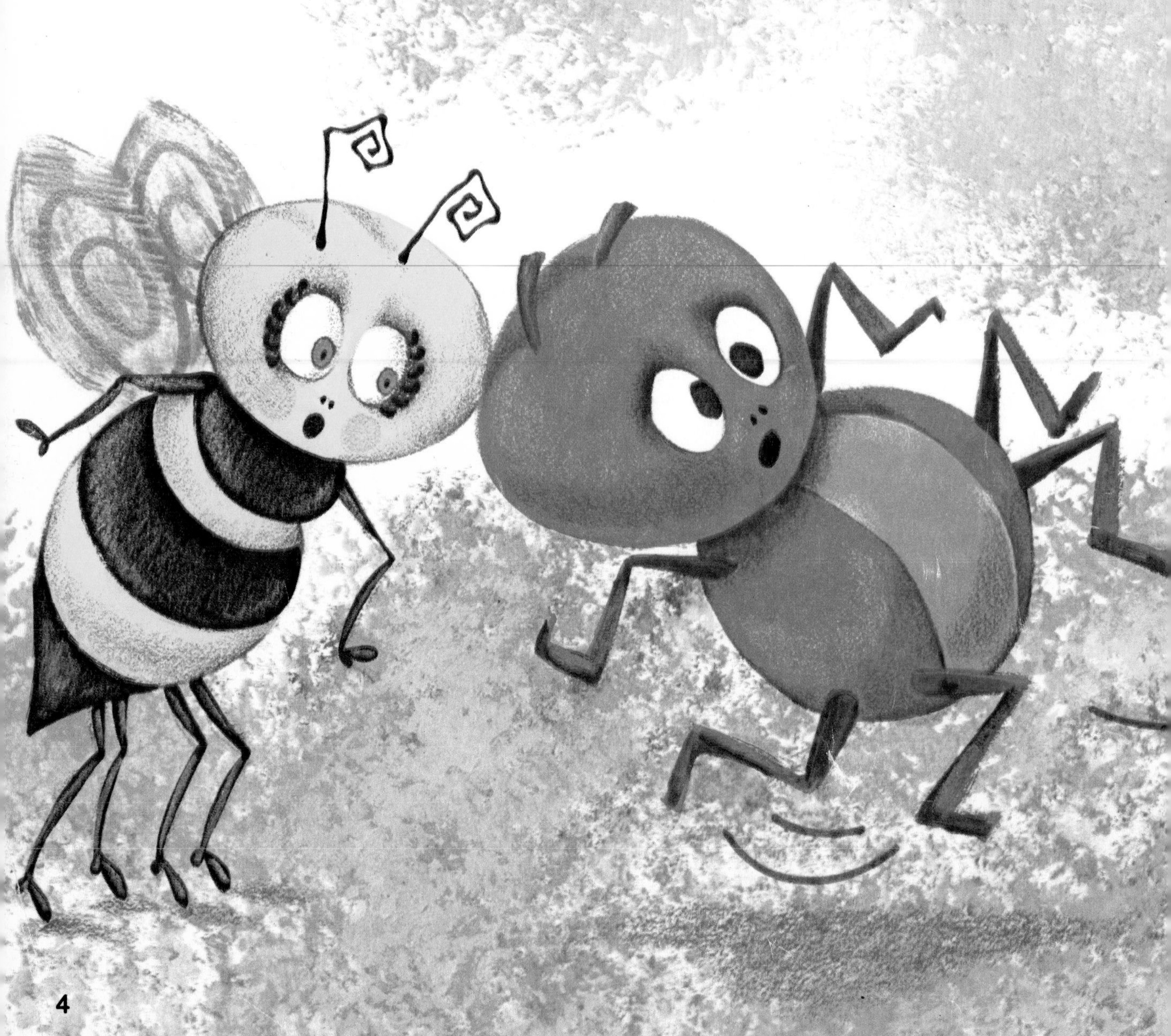

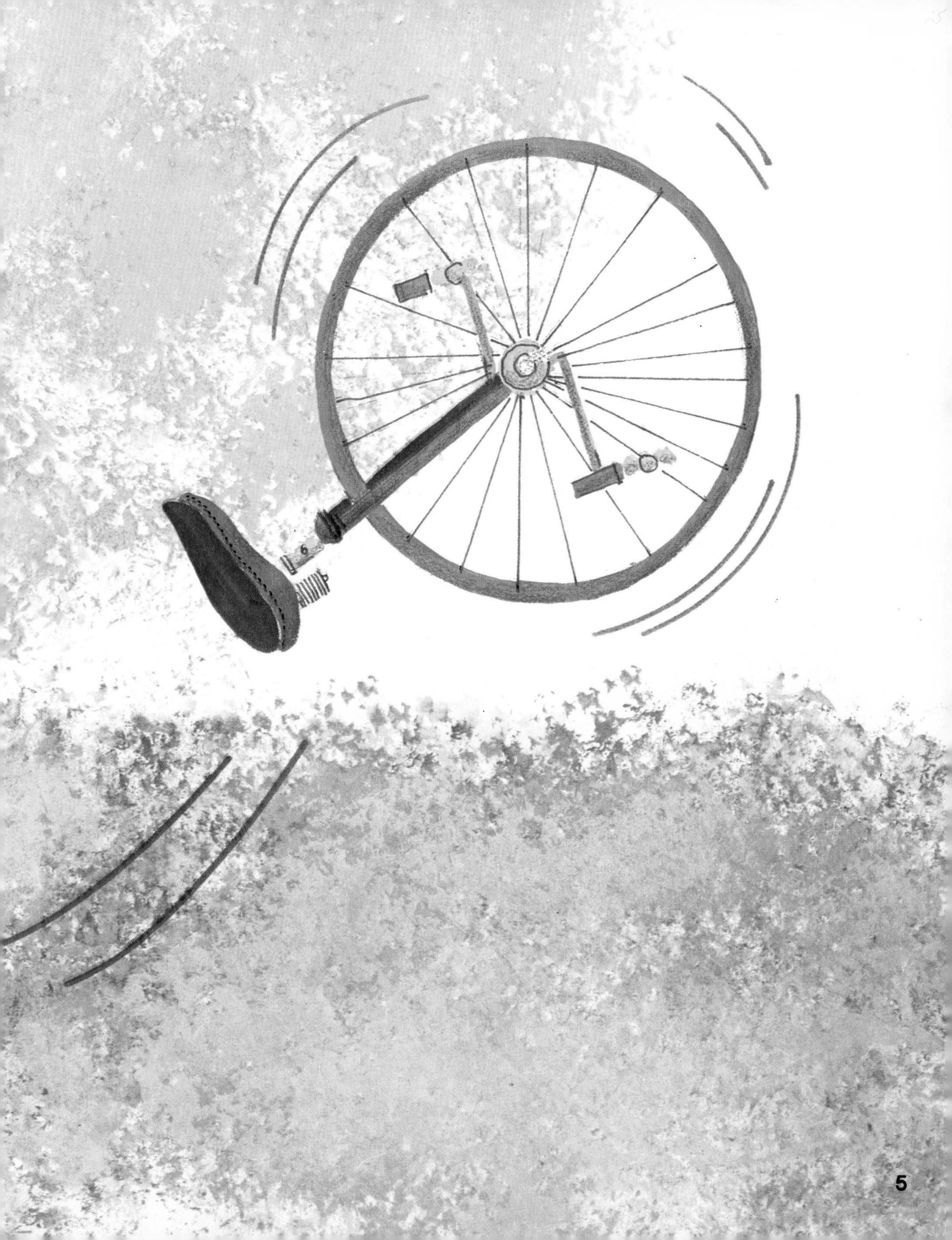

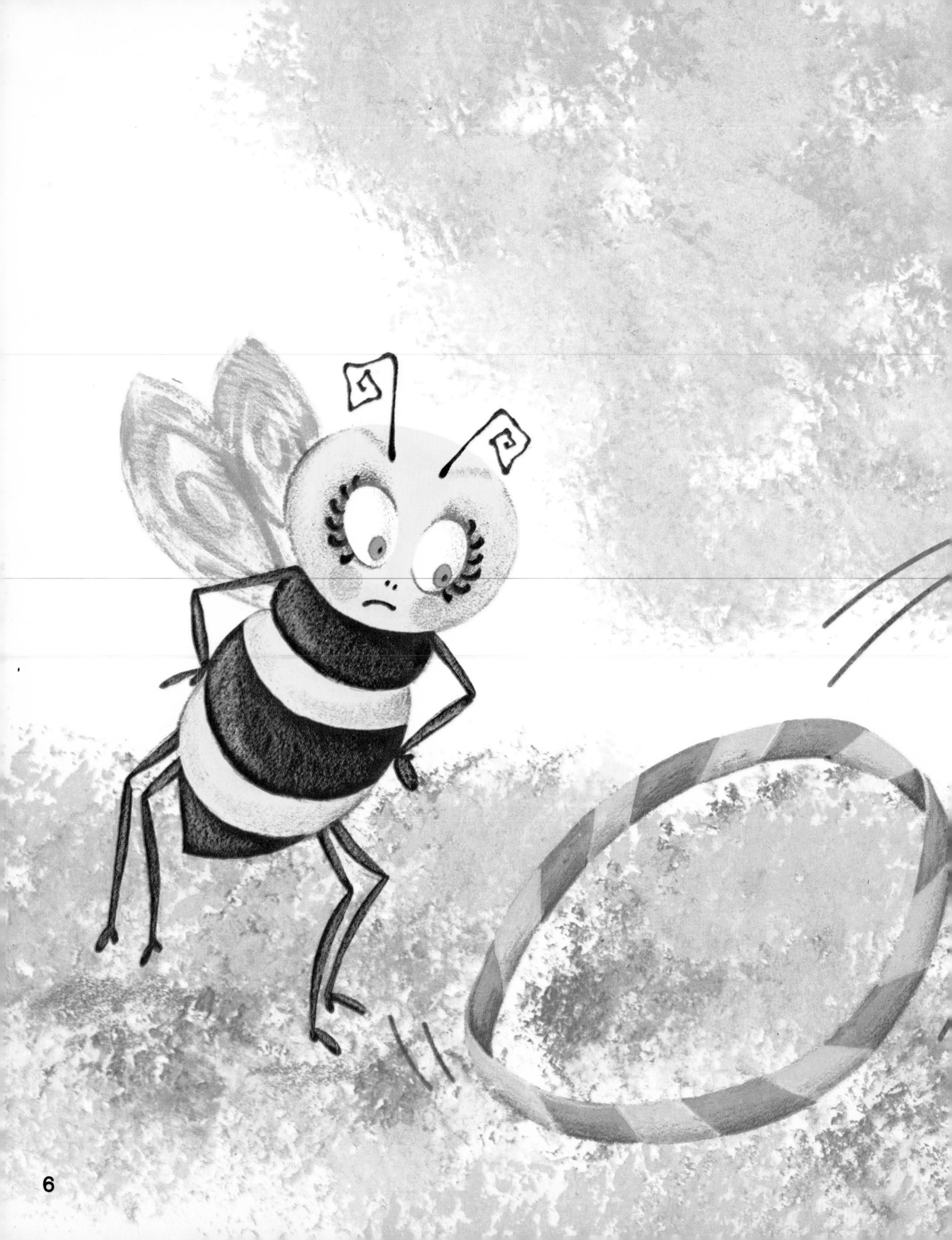

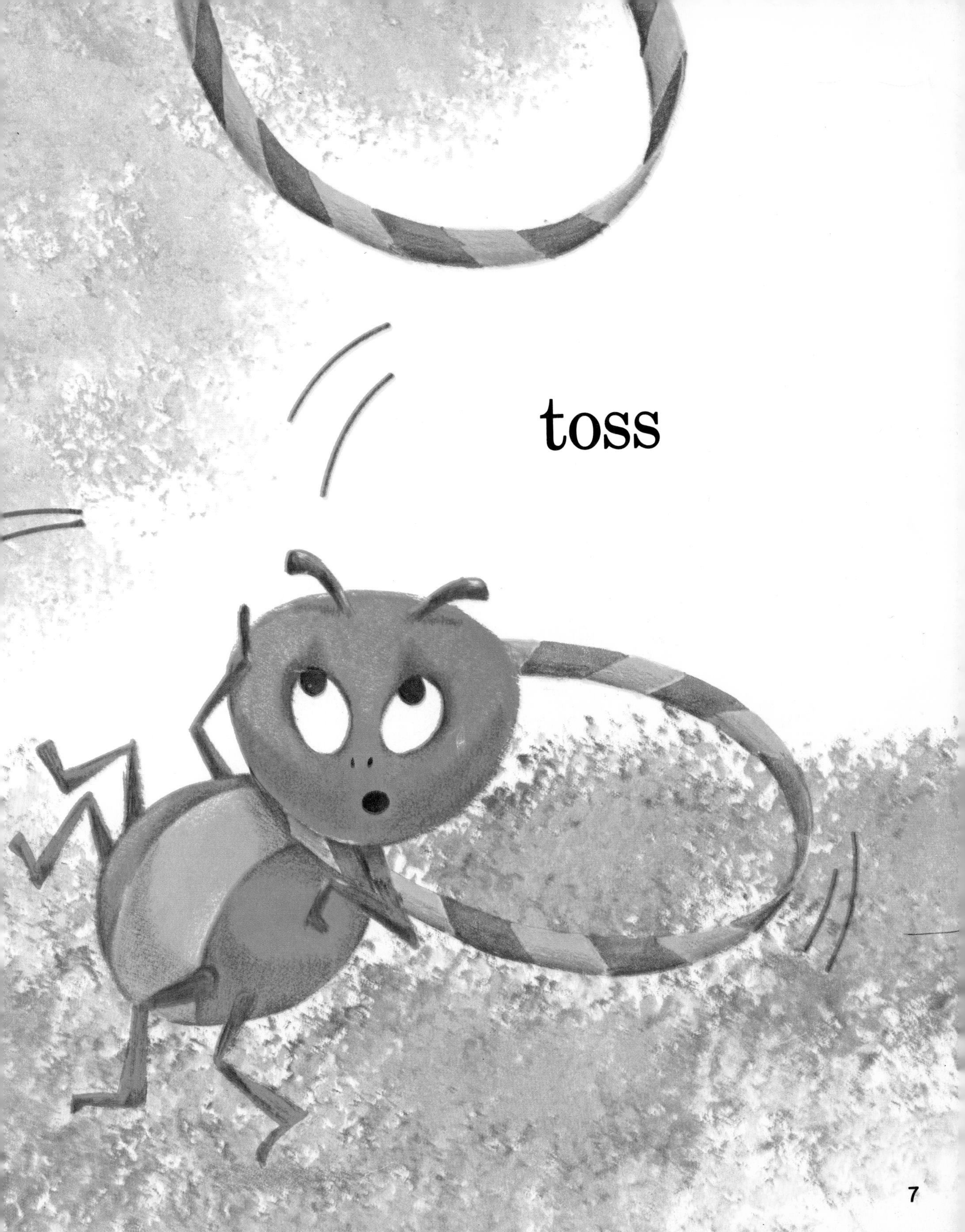

toss

roll

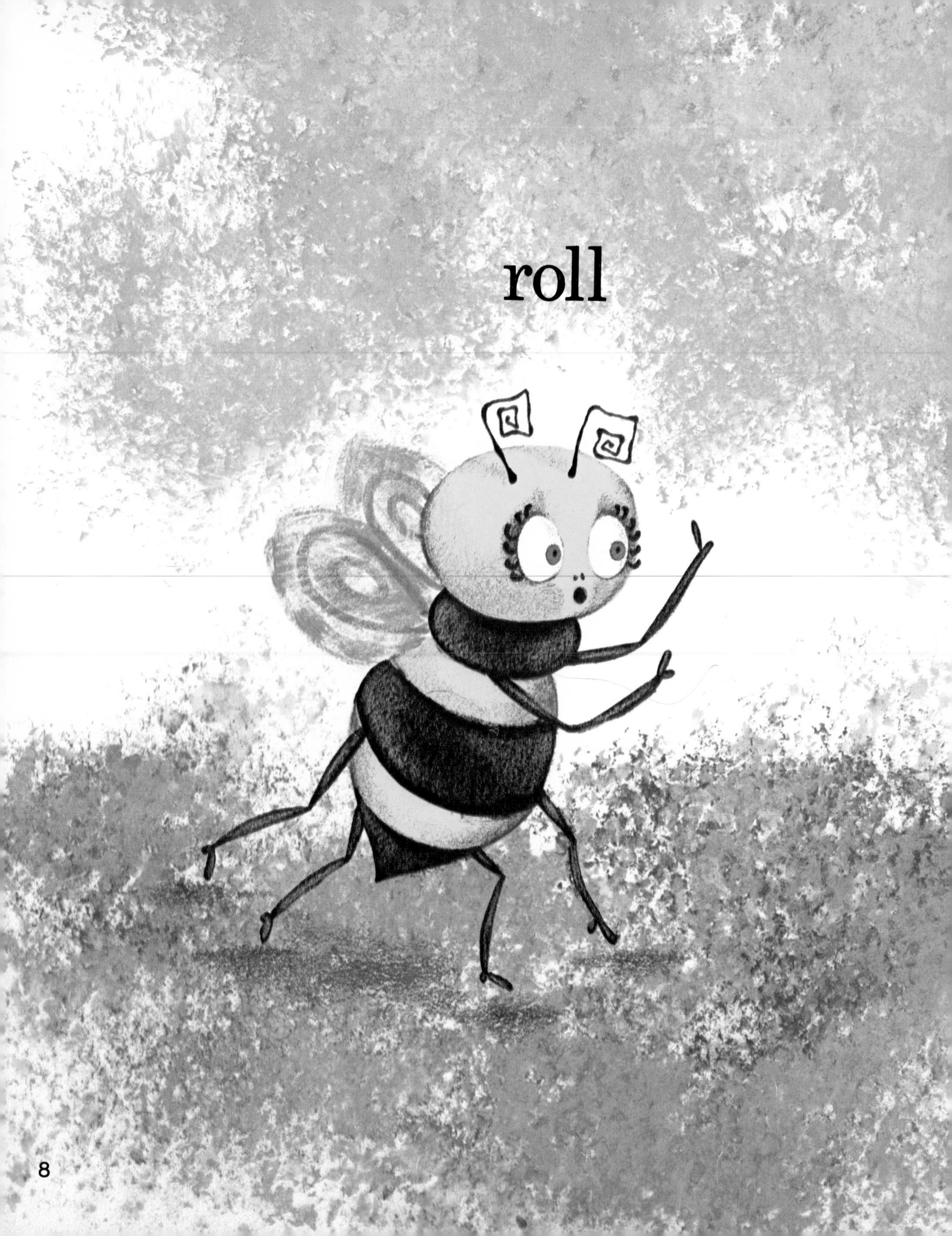

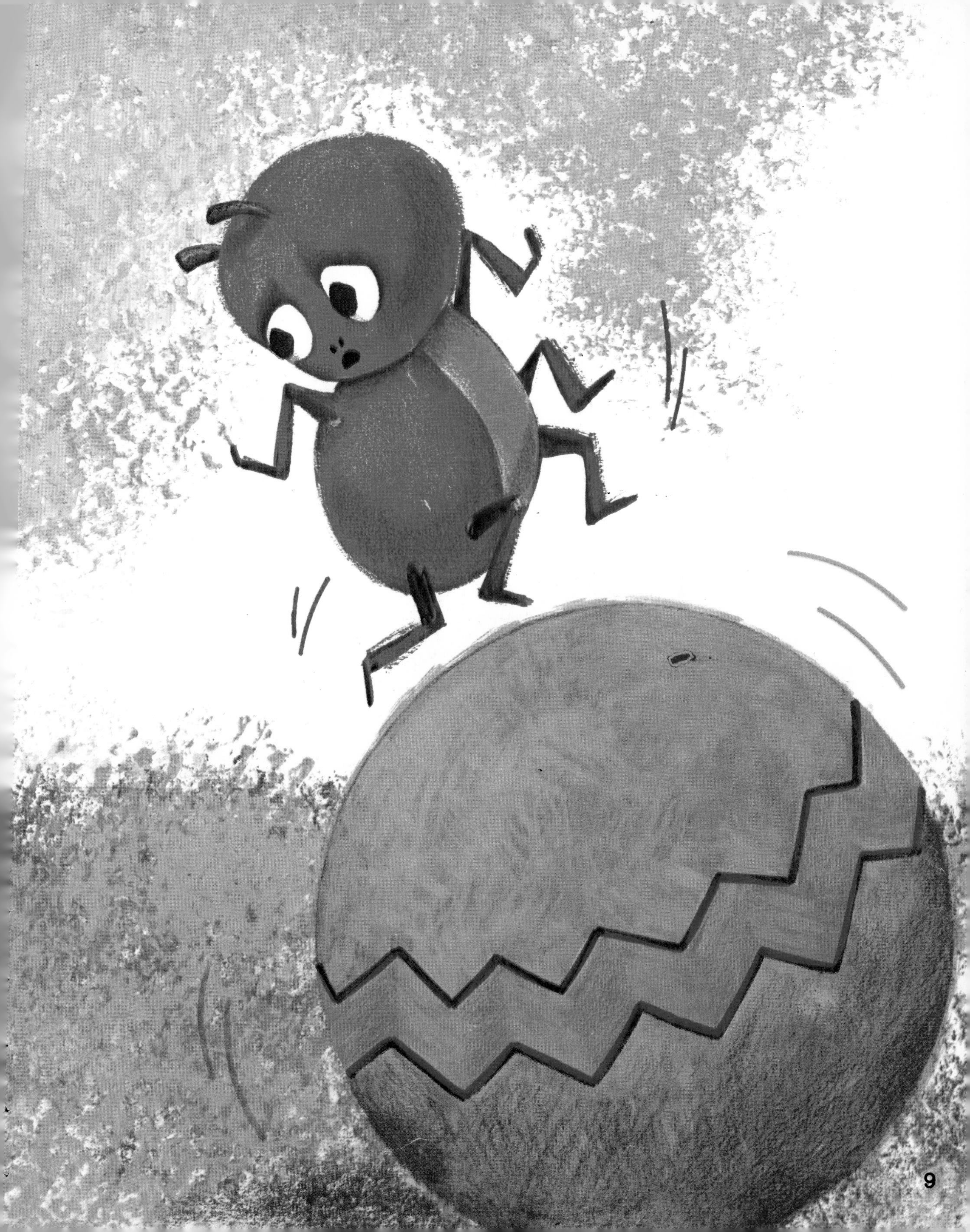

lift

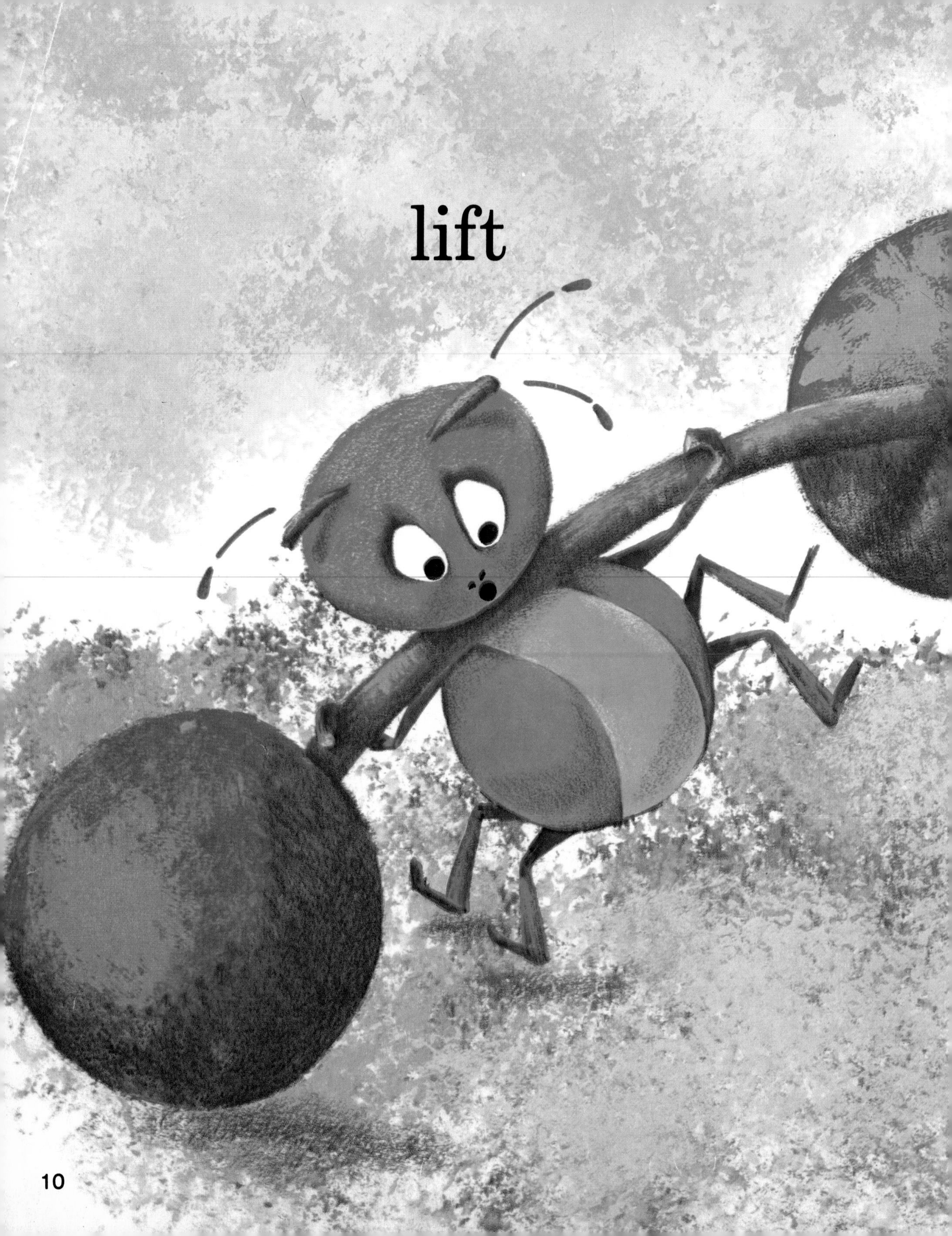

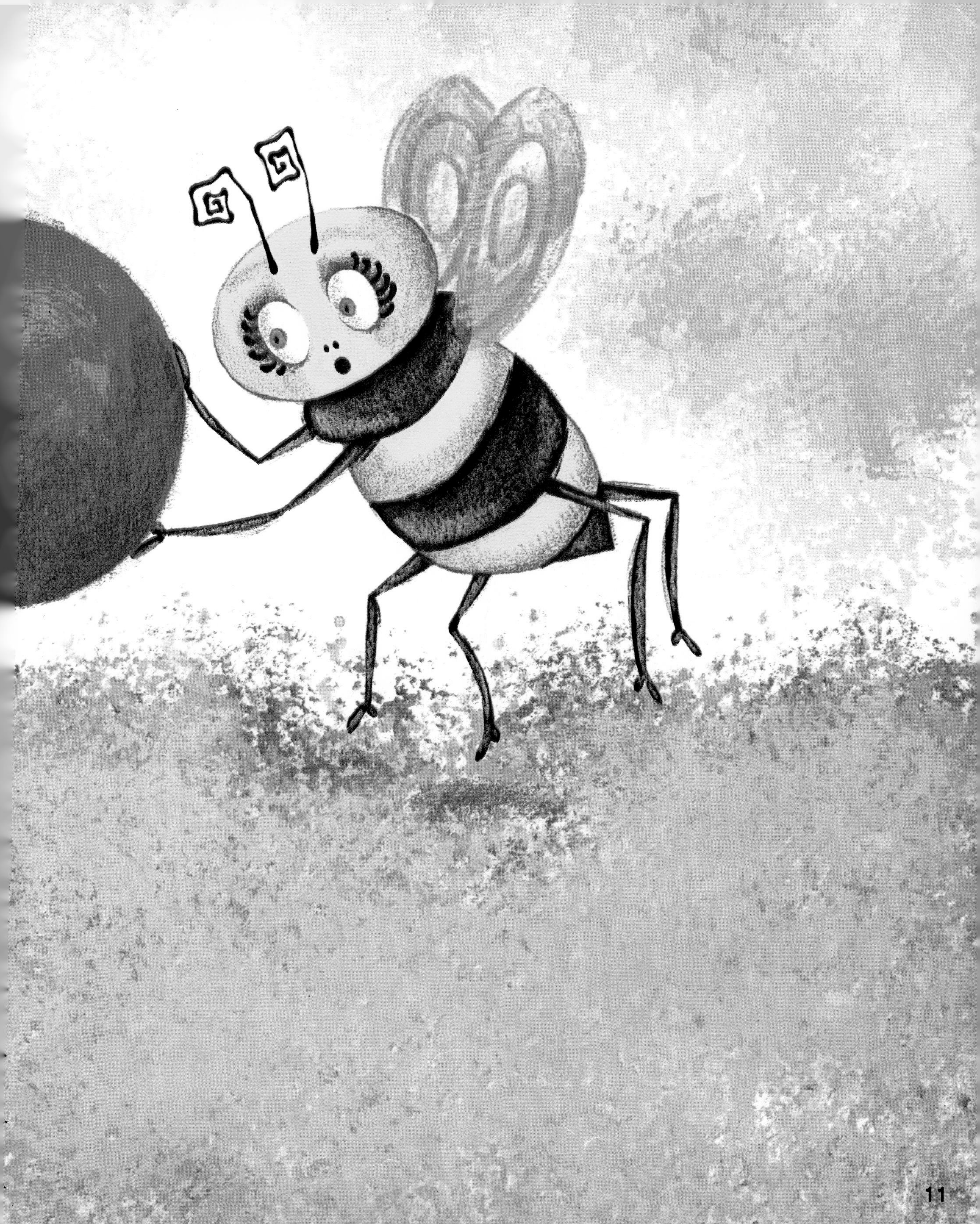

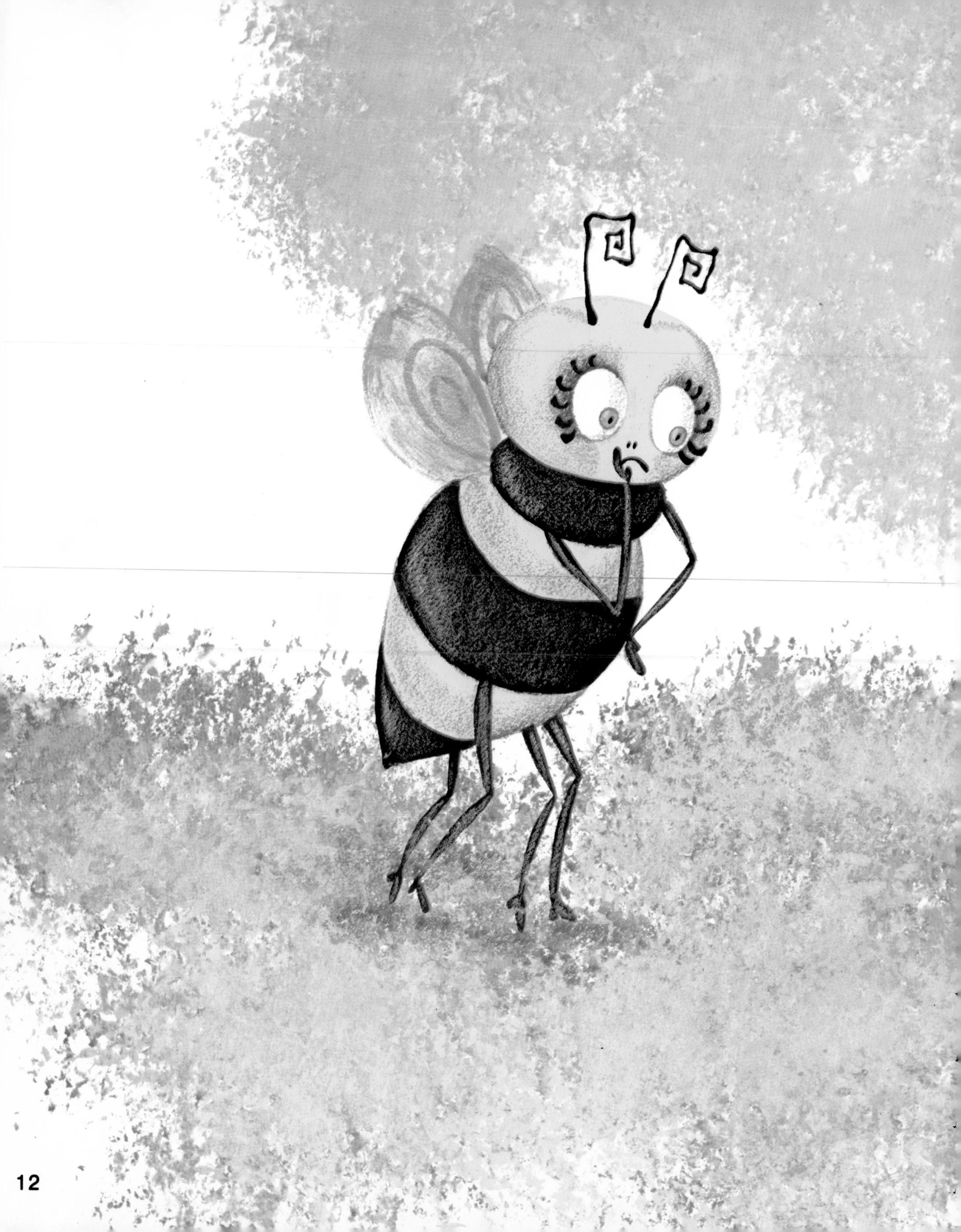

play

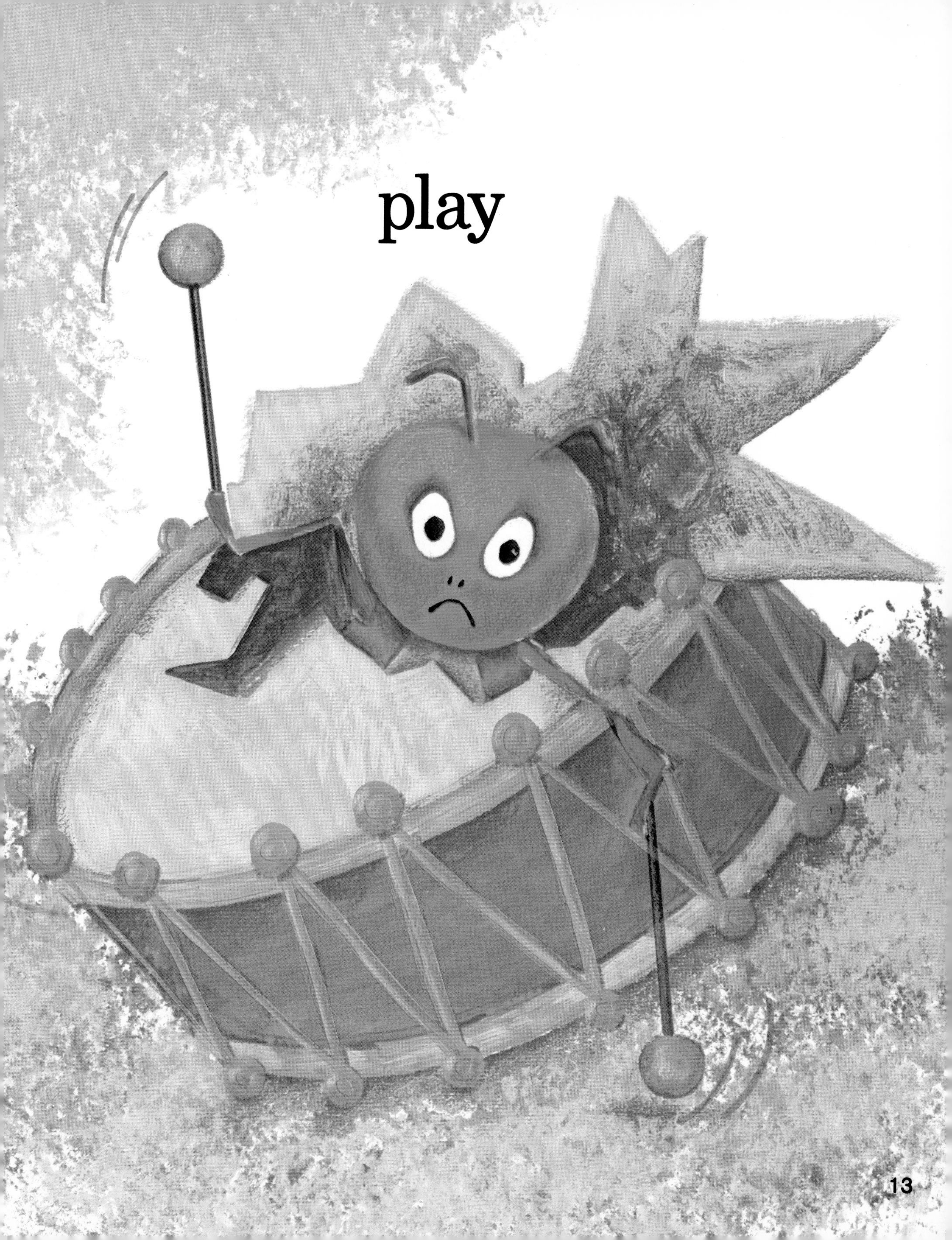

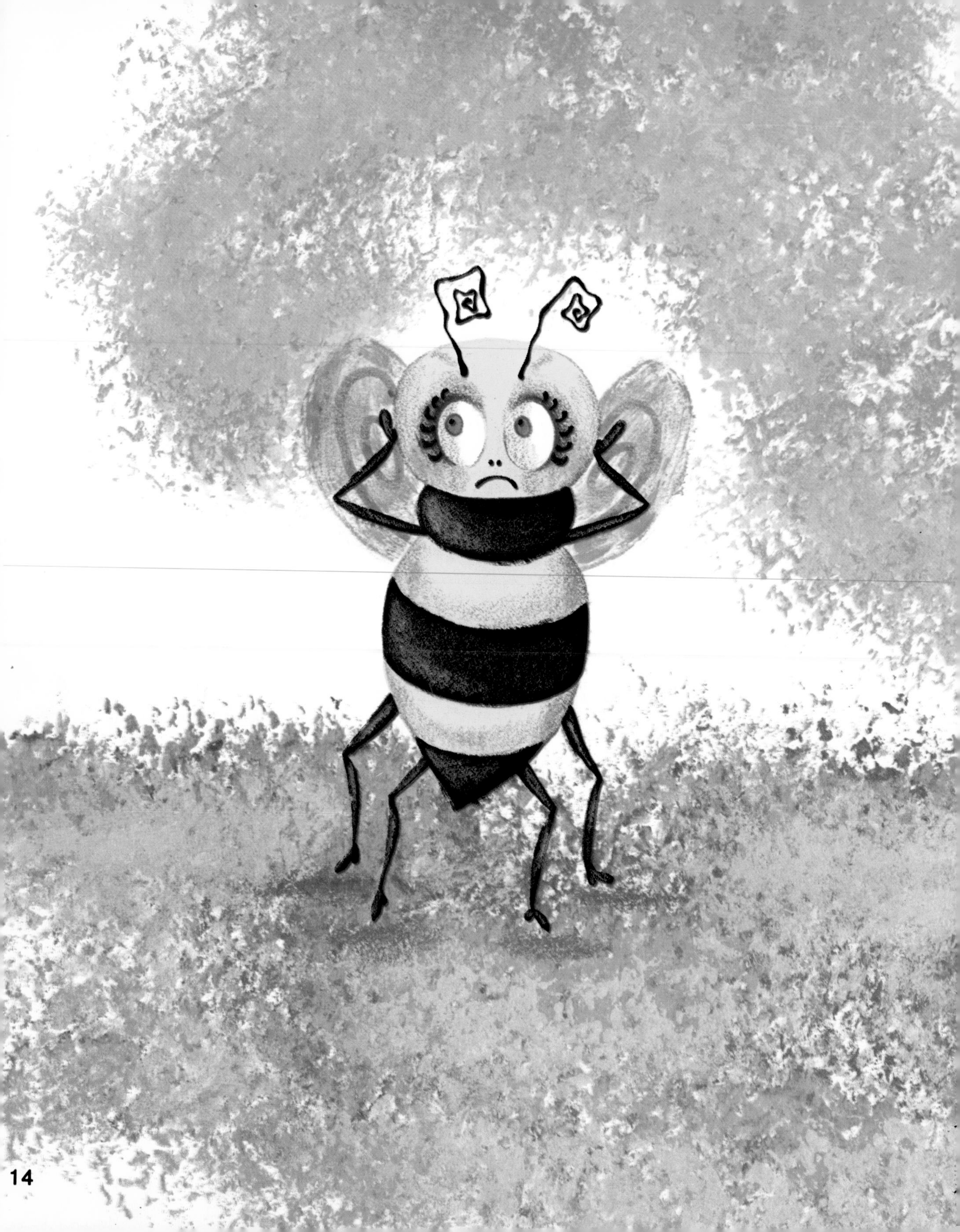

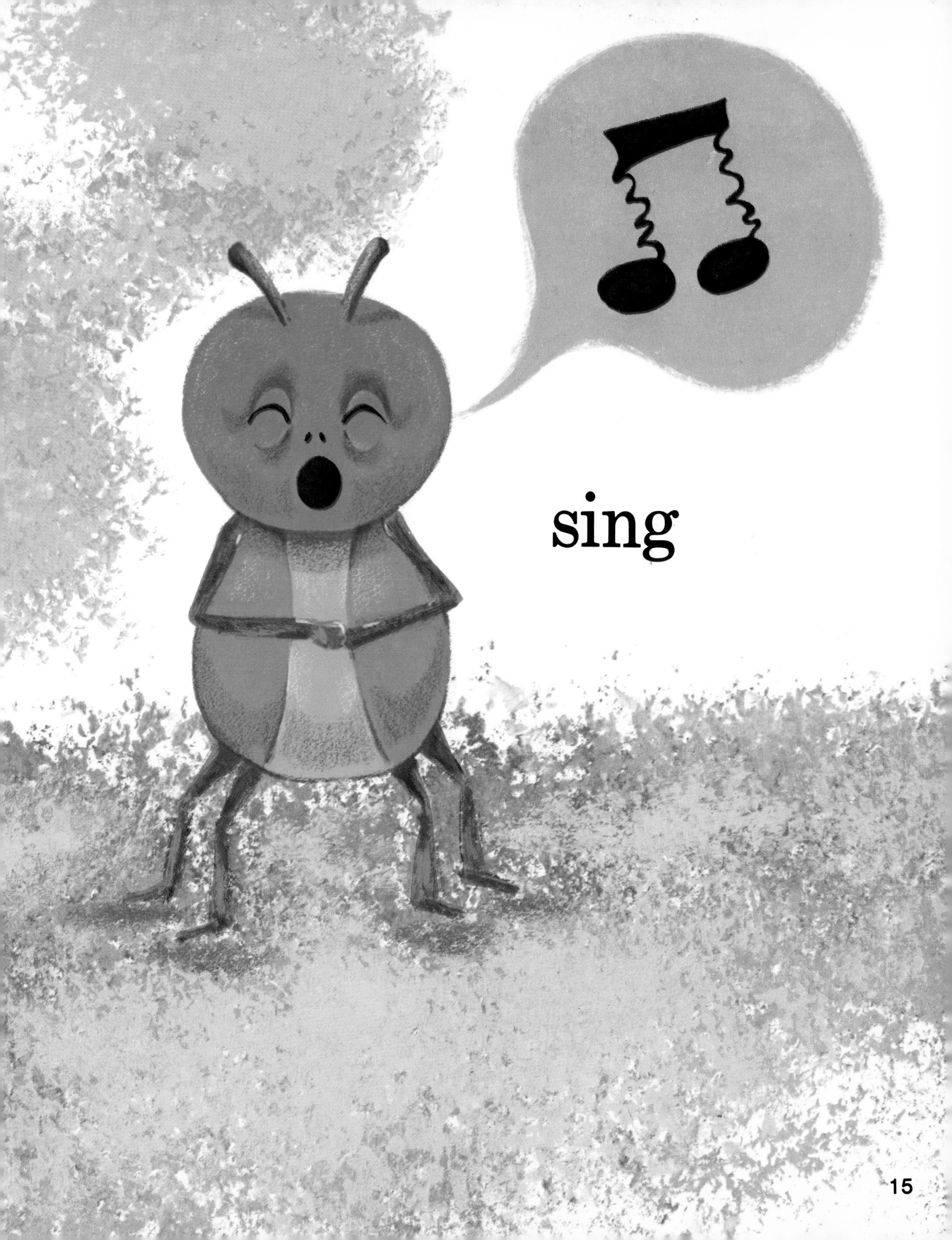

sing

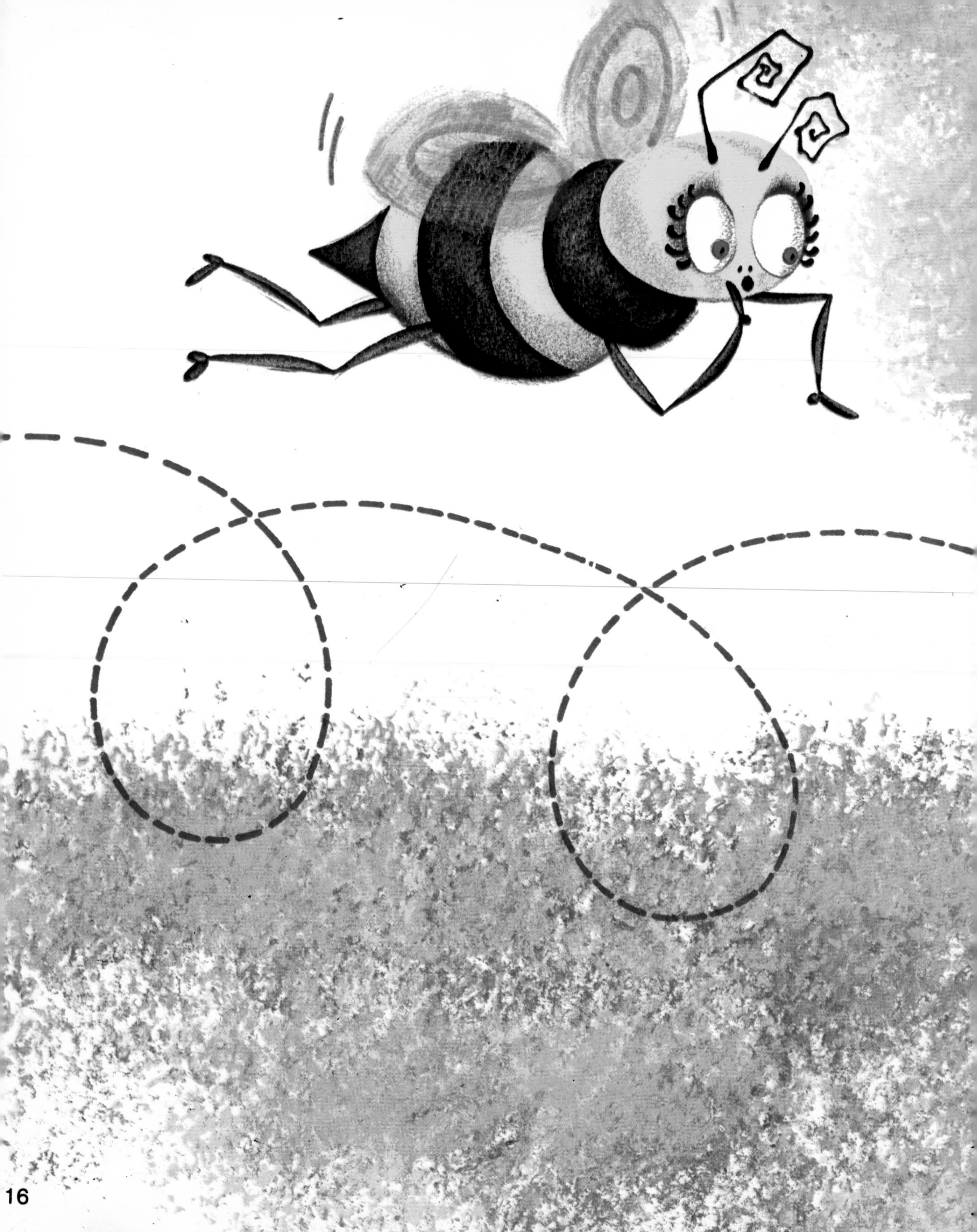

tumble

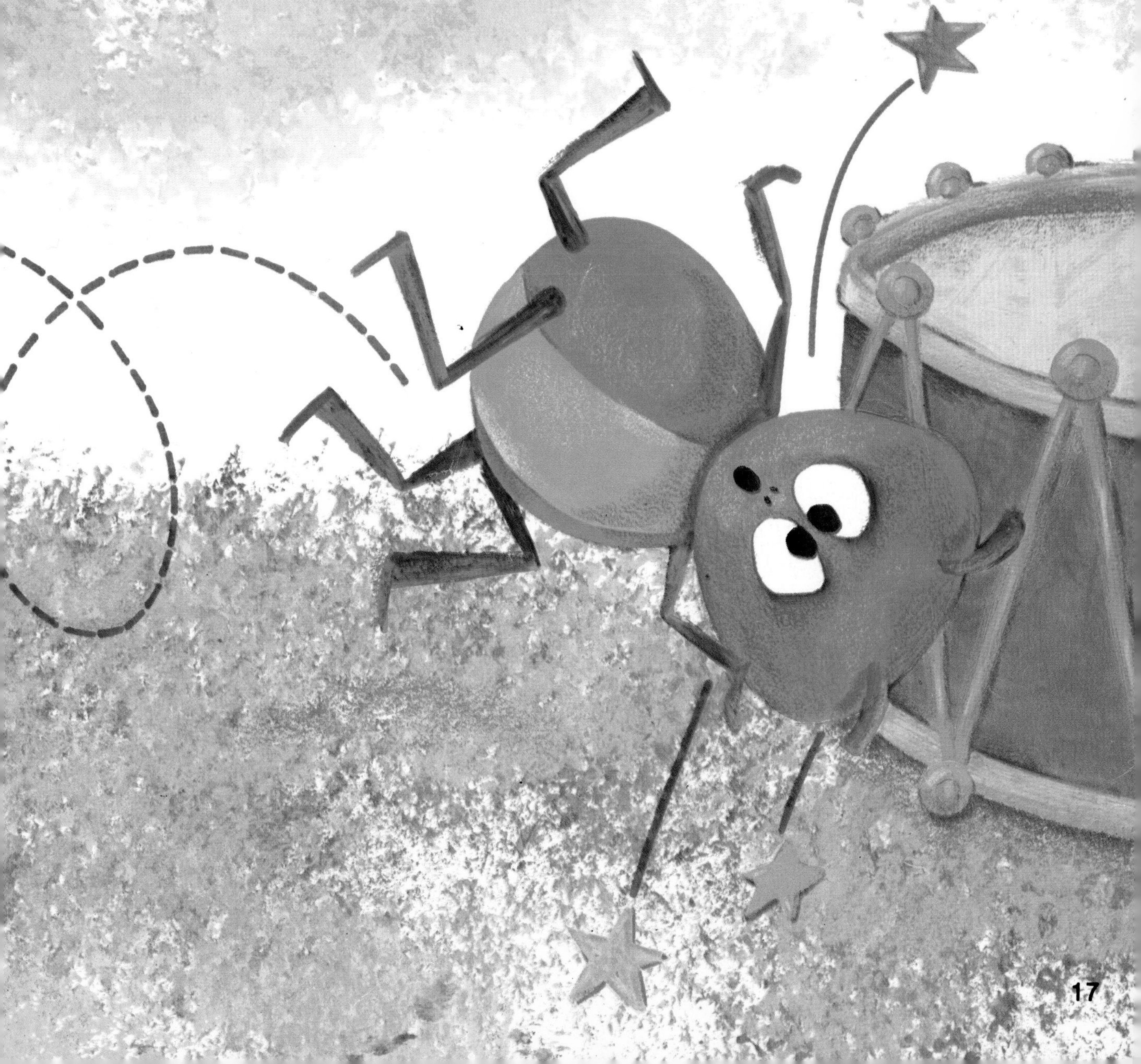

march

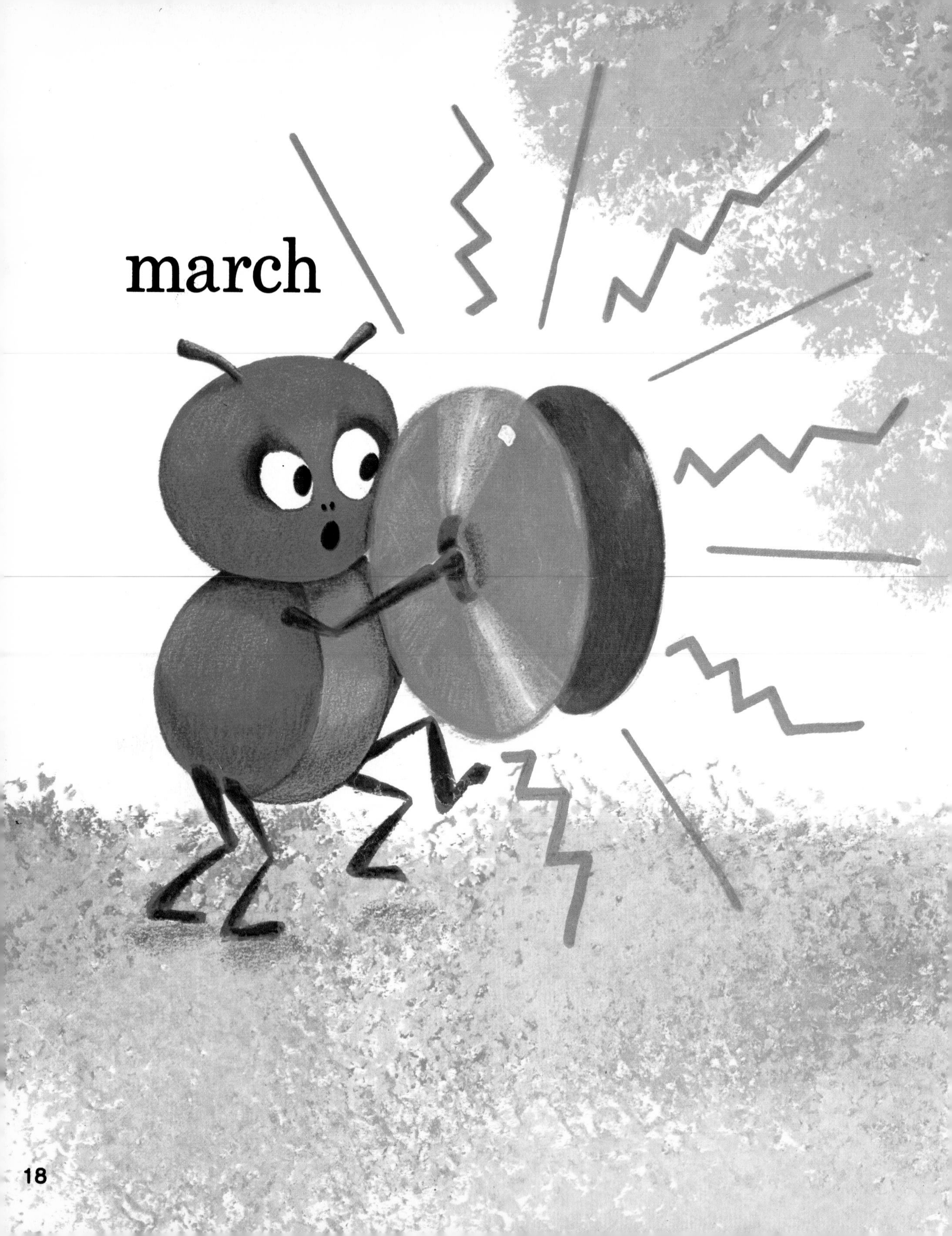

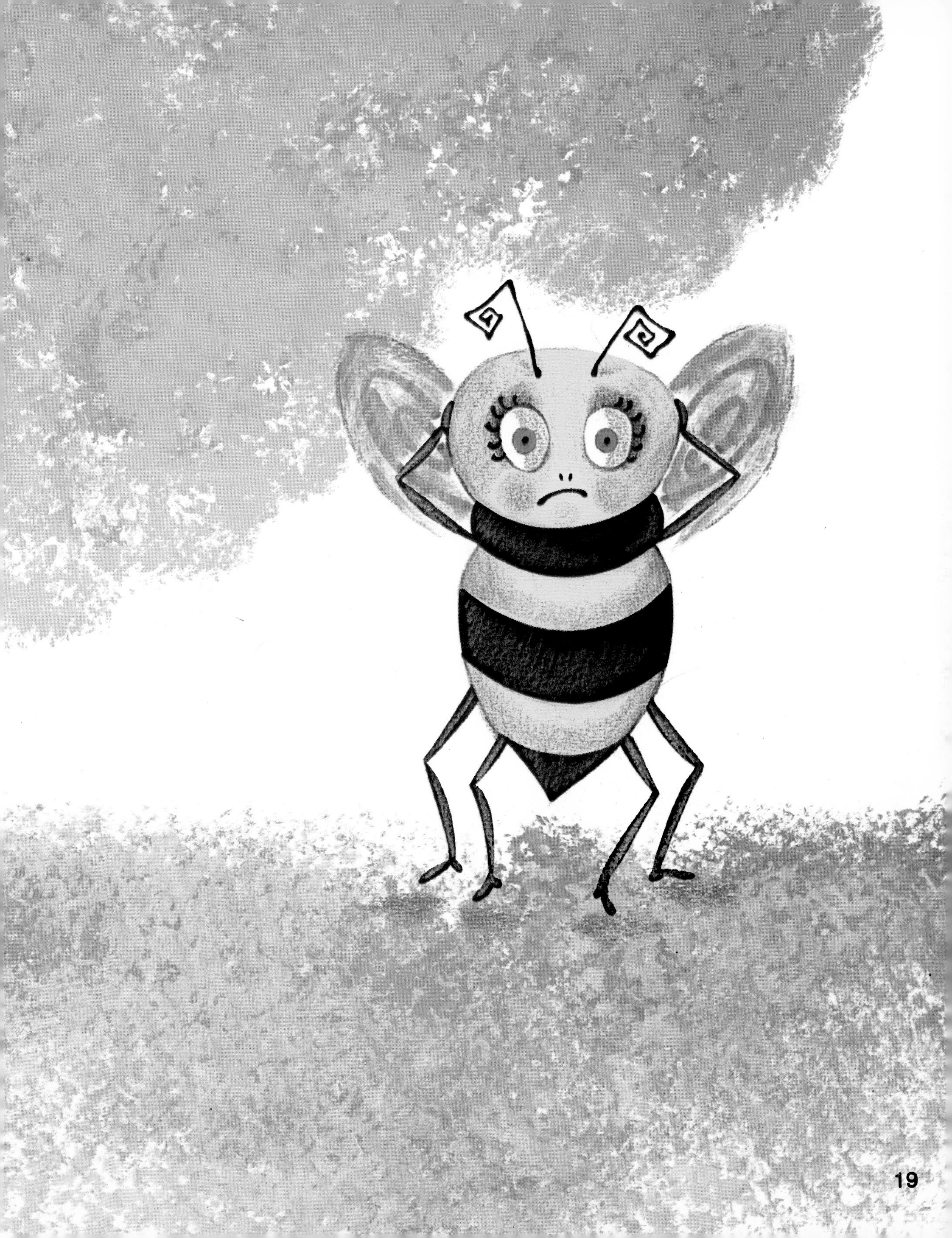

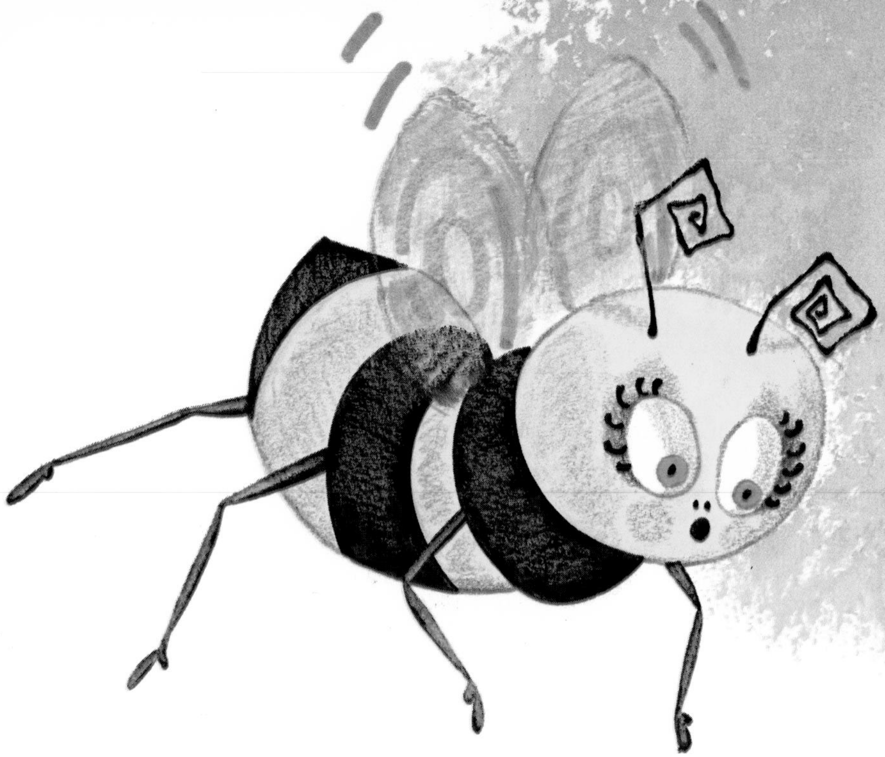

swing

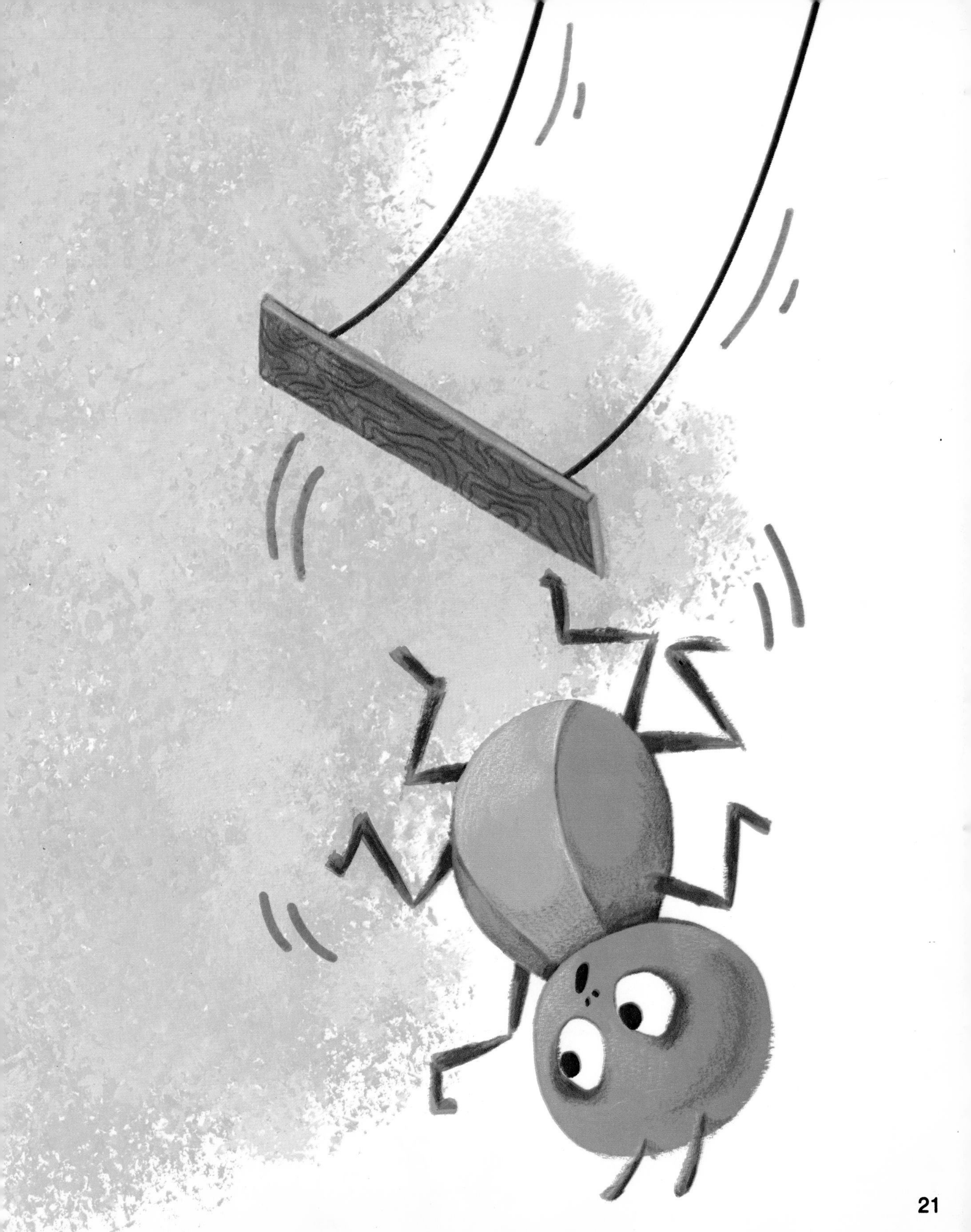

# juggle

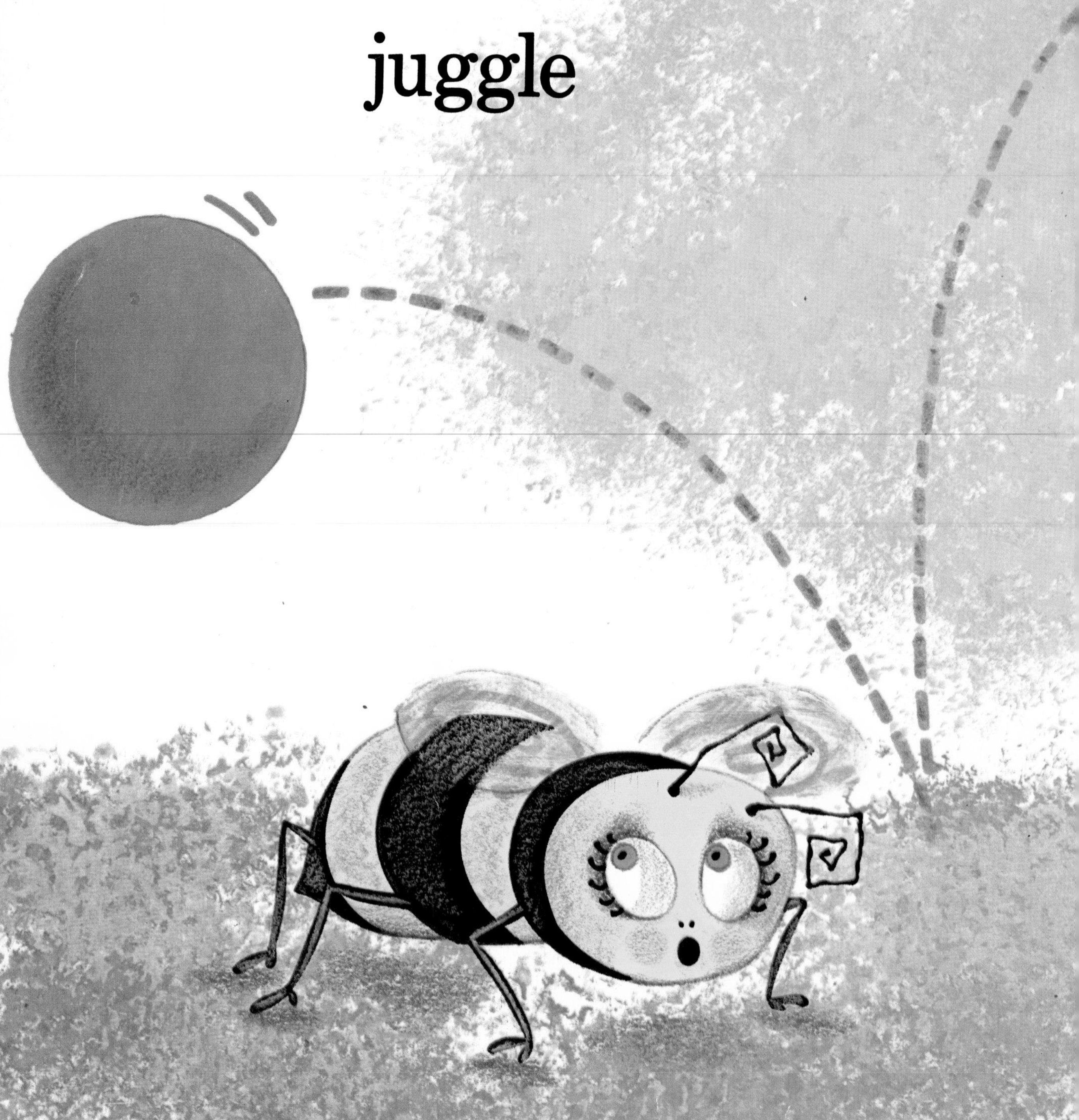

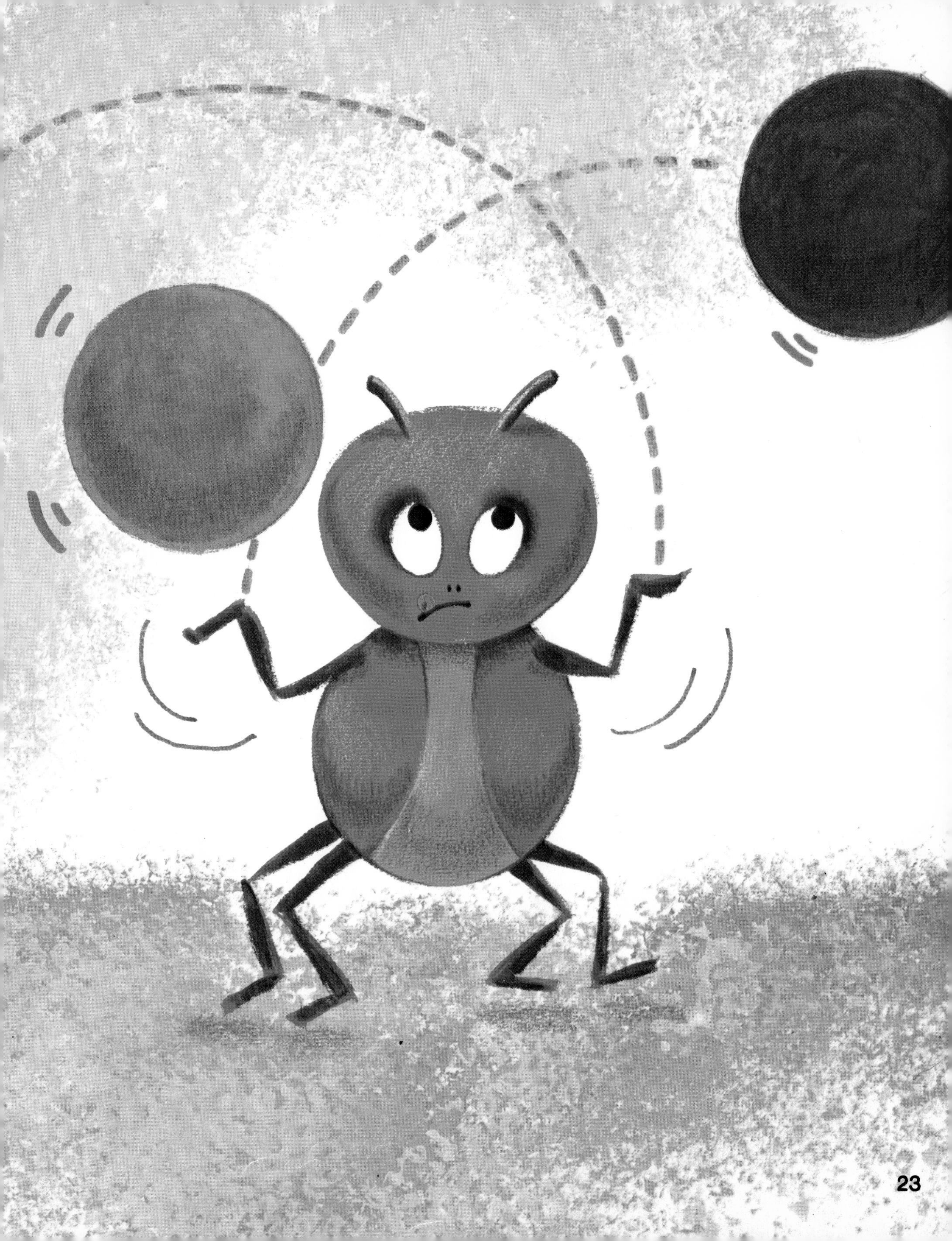

balance ... and

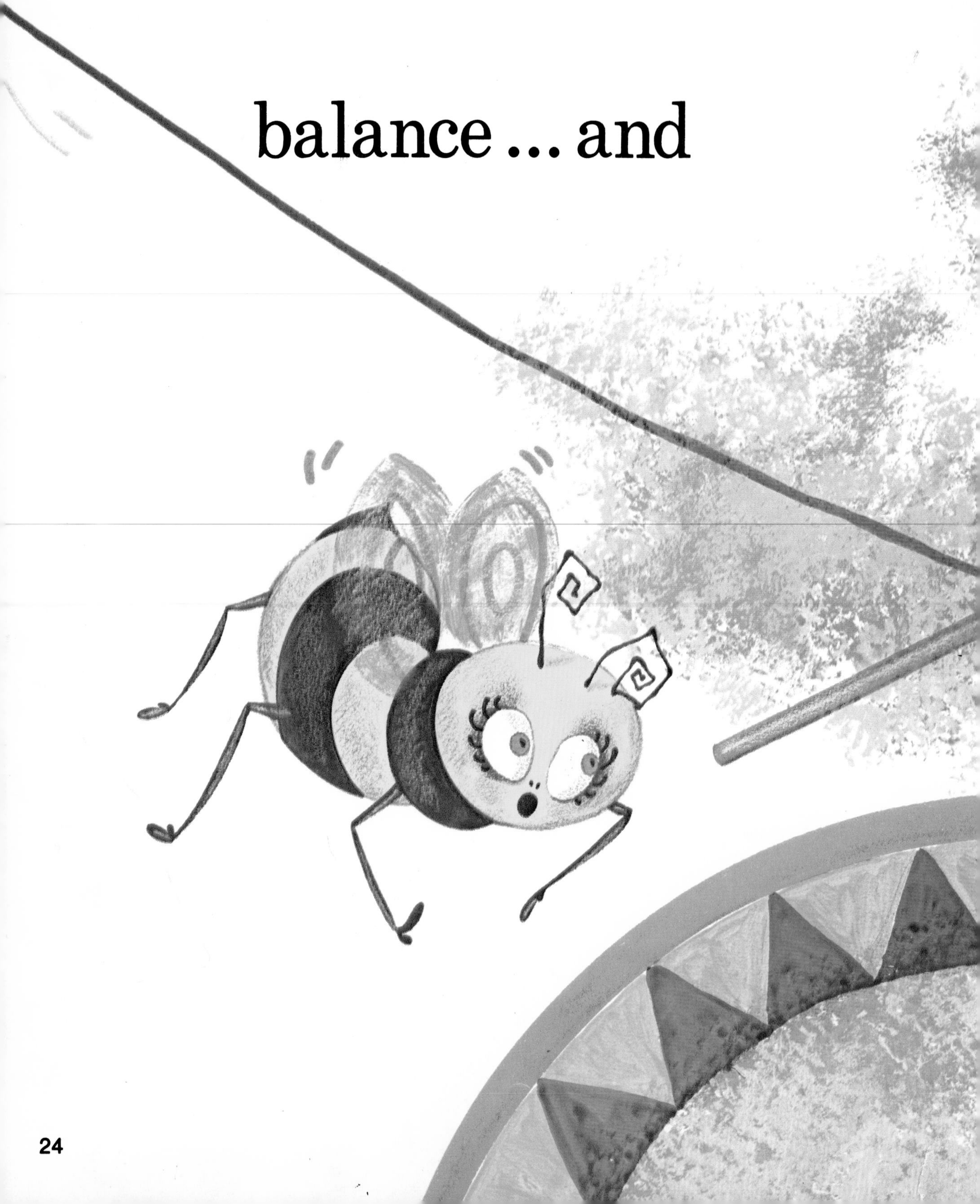

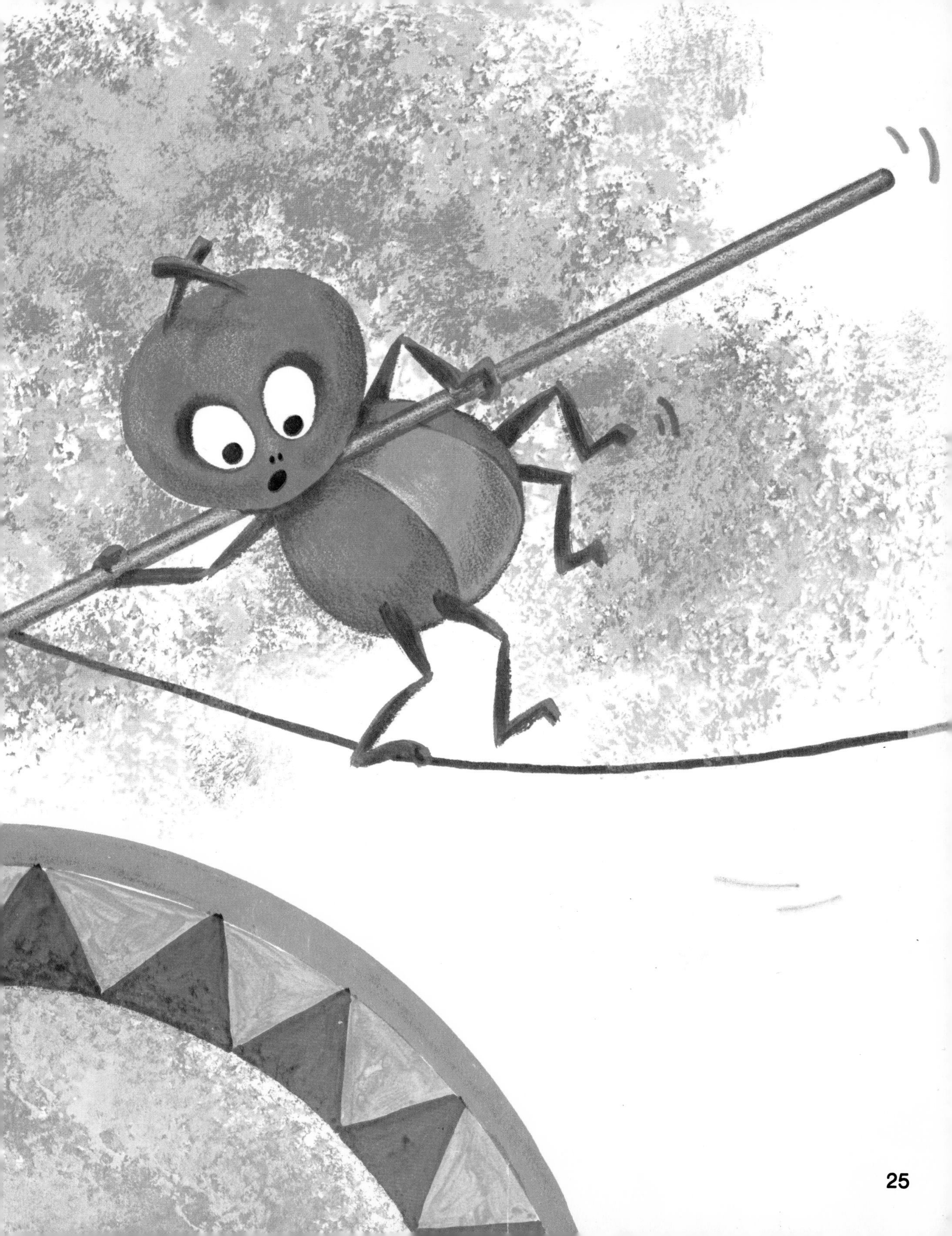

be brave.

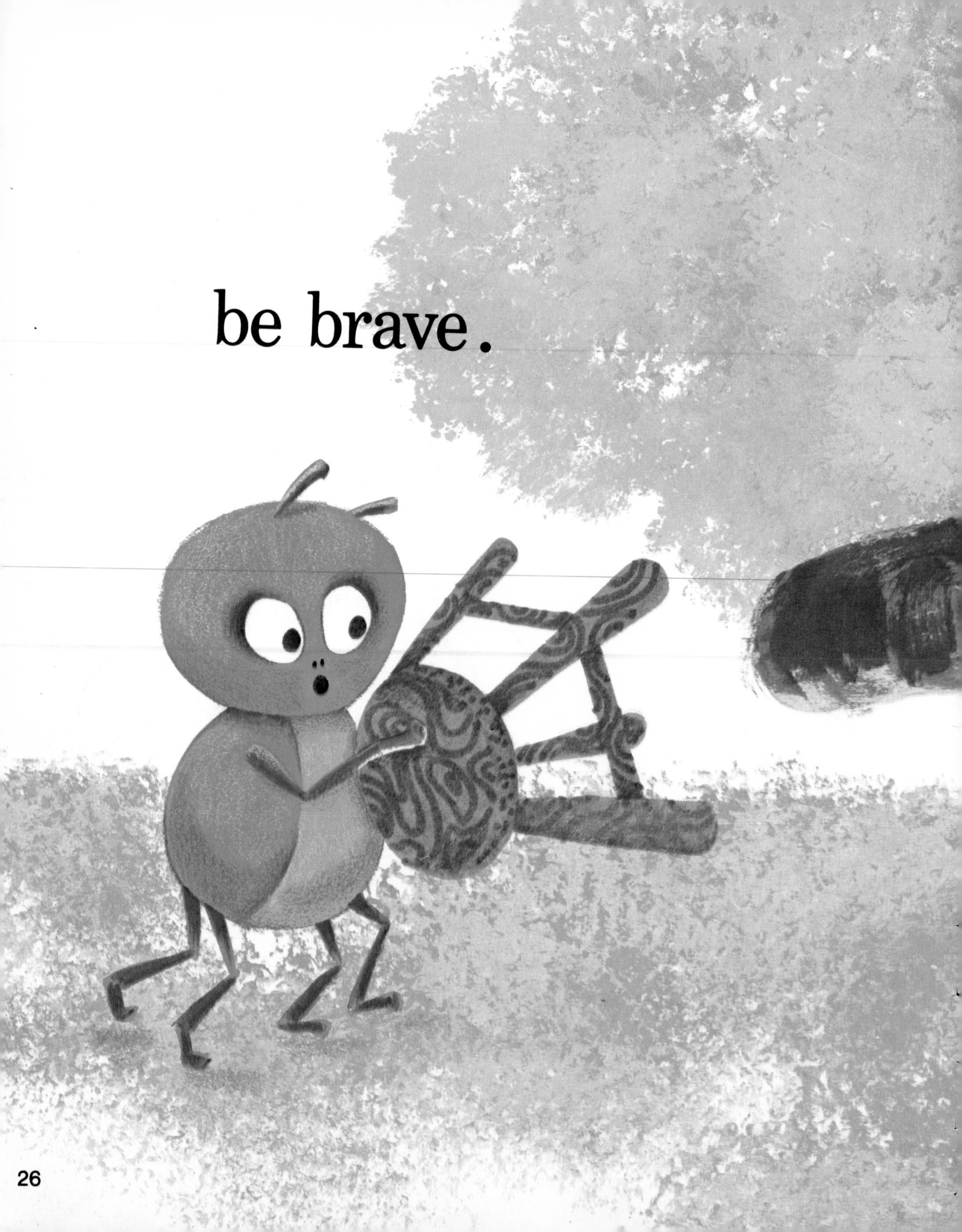

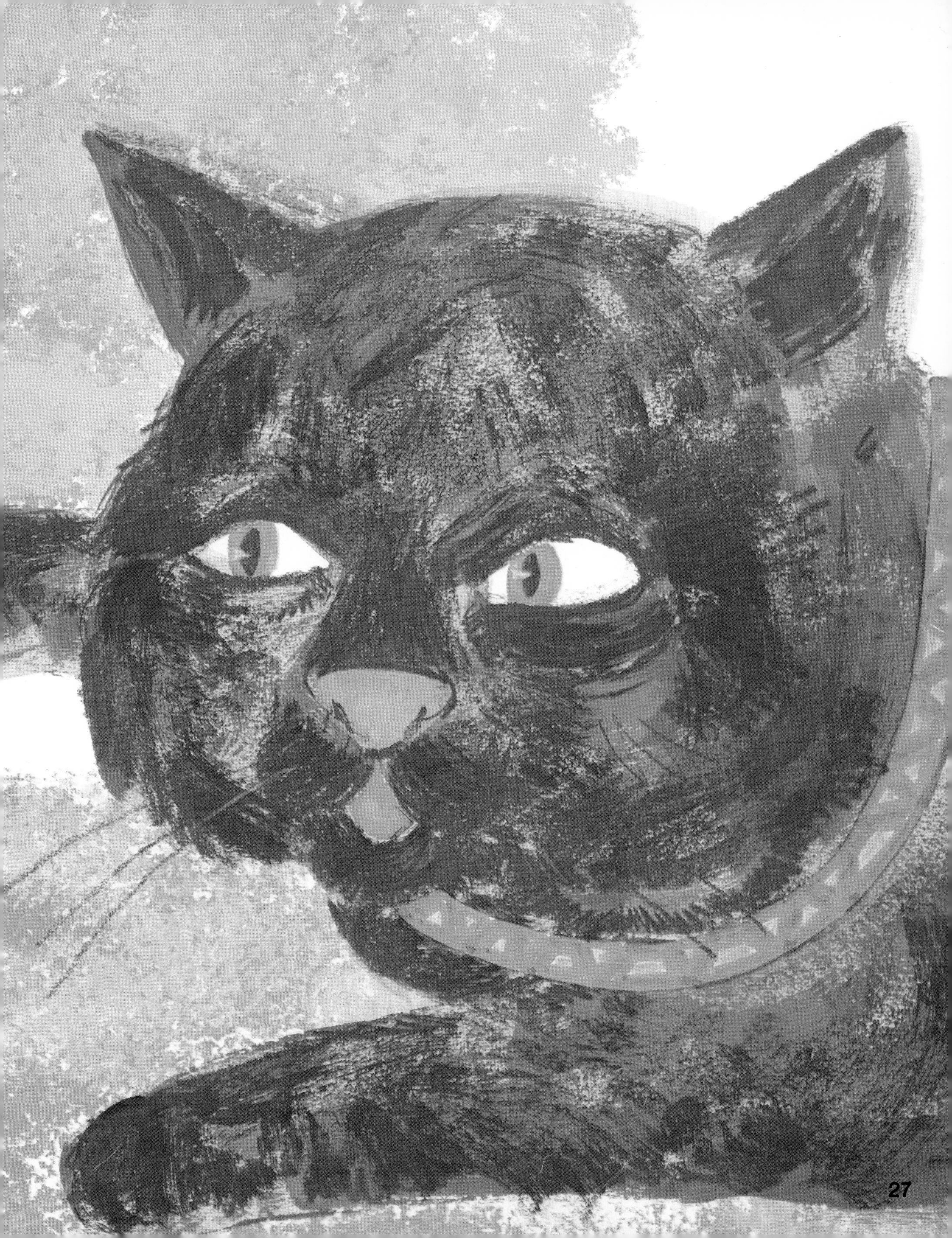

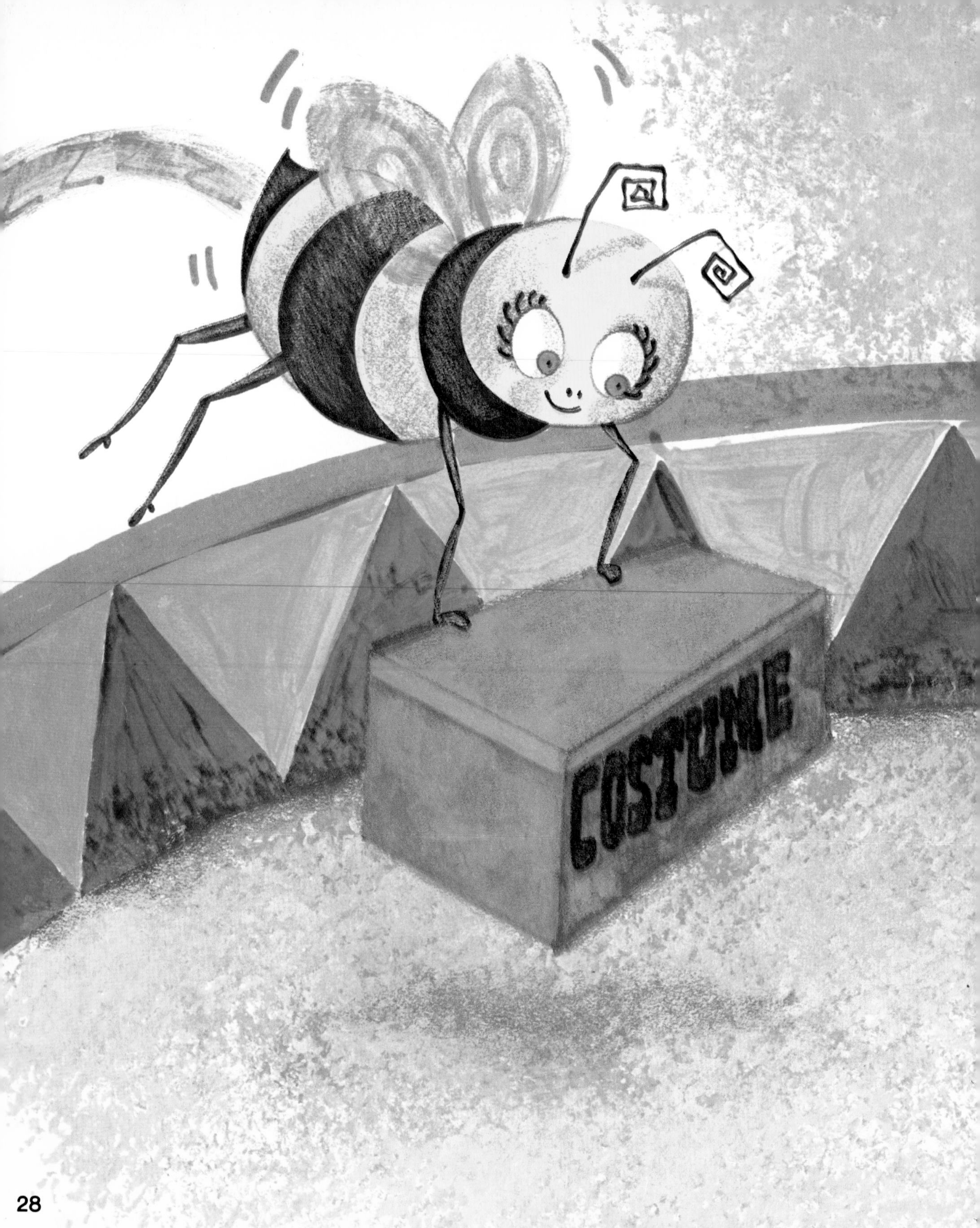
COSTUME

# Then Feebee

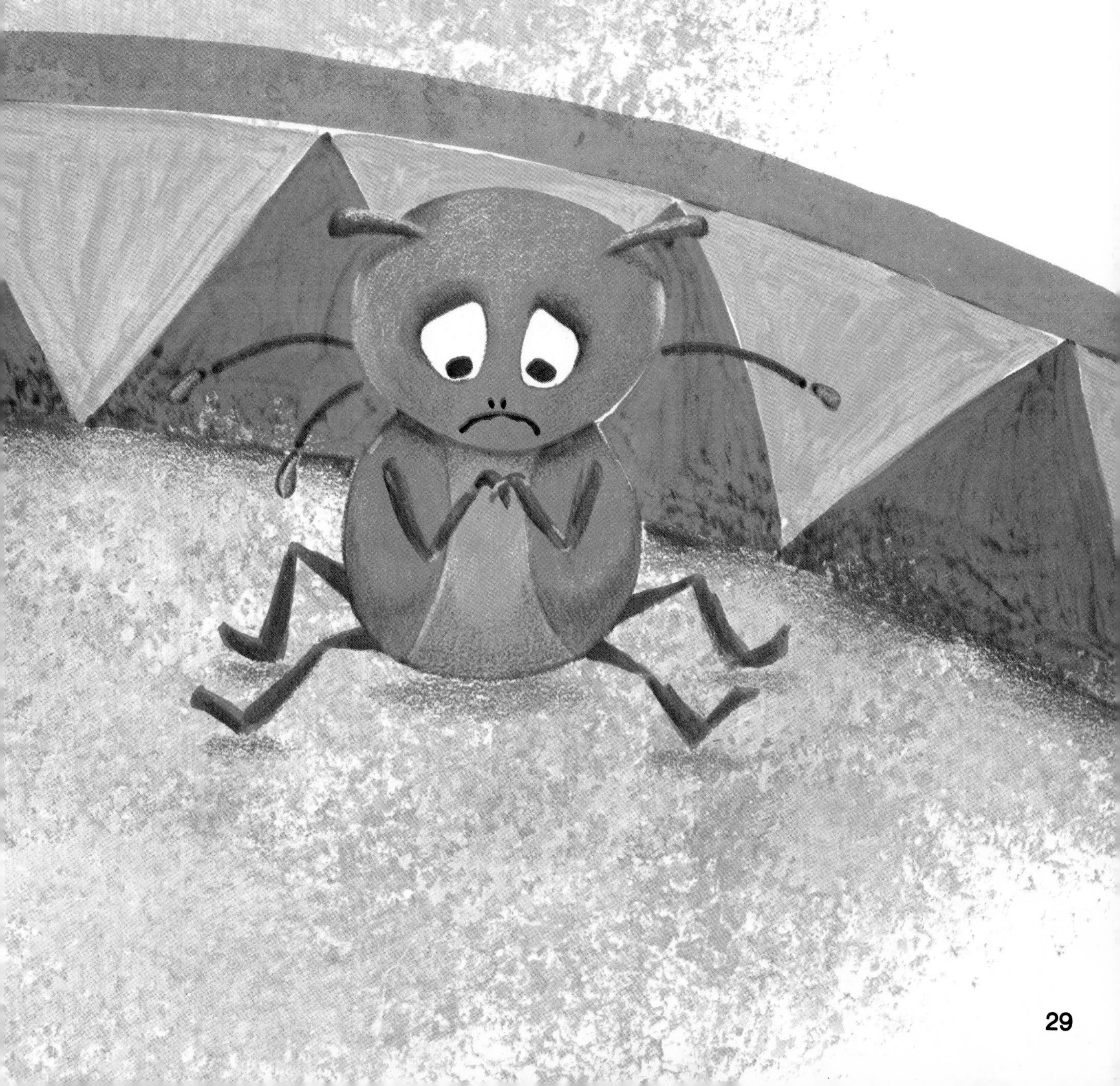

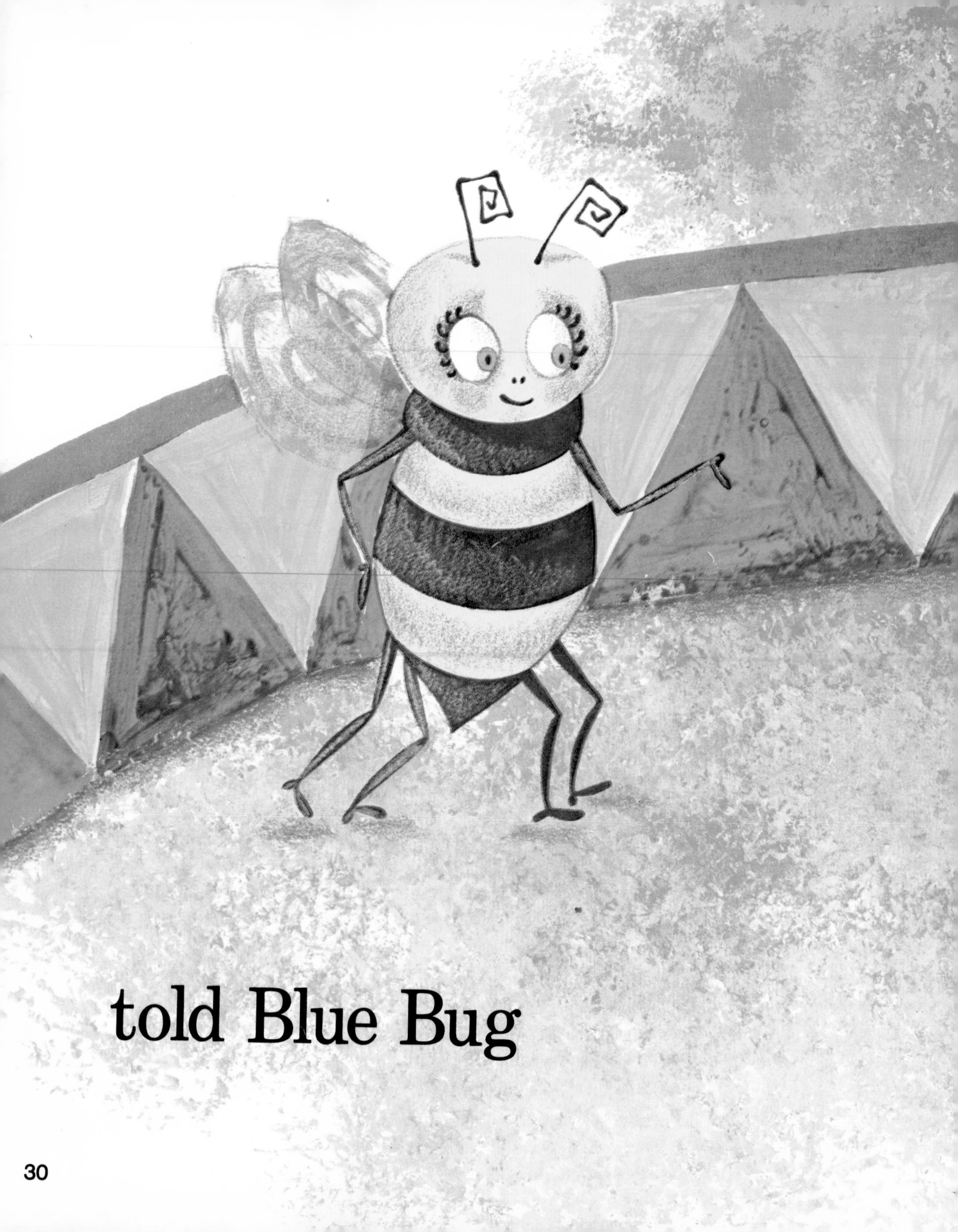

told Blue Bug

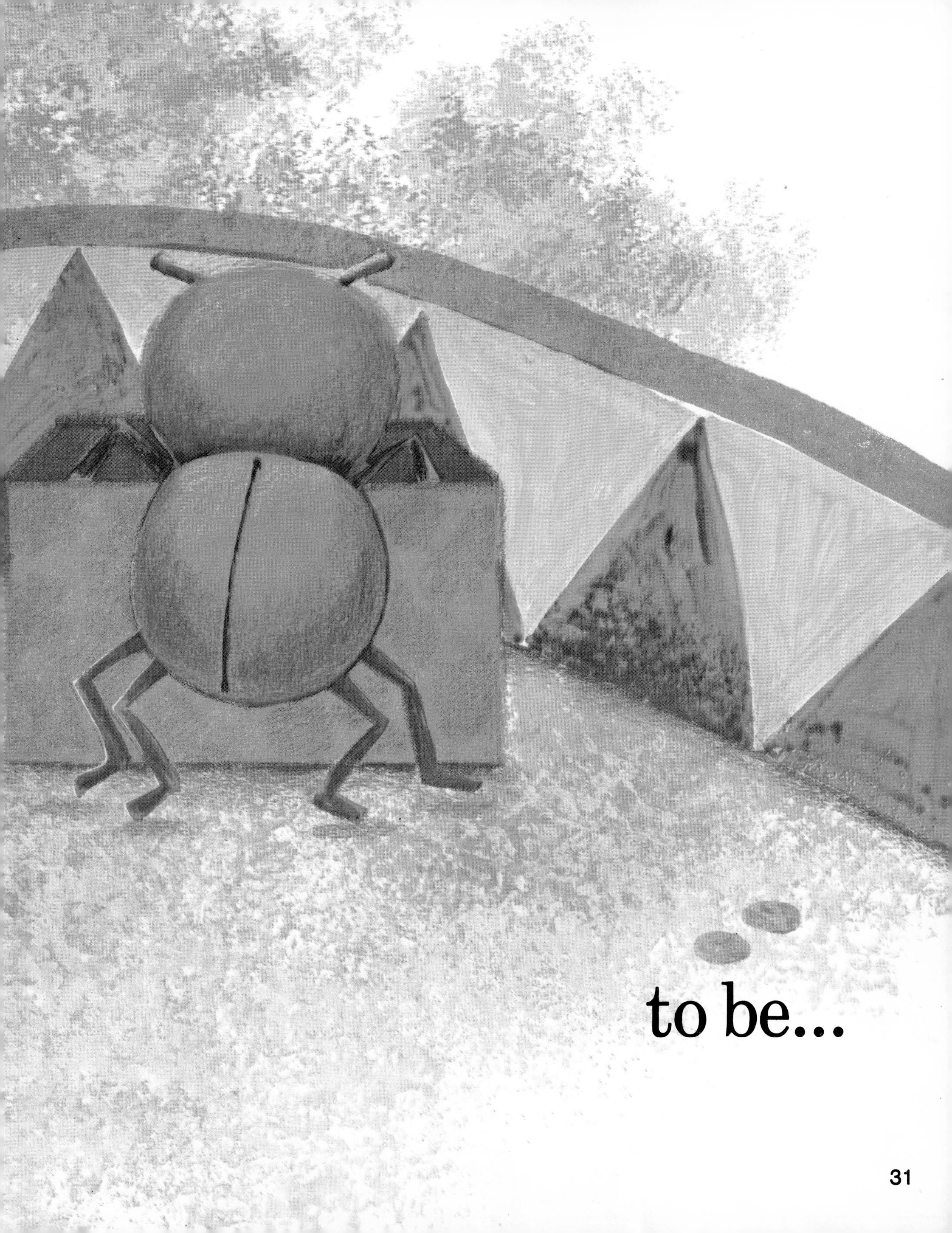

to be...

# the CLOWN!

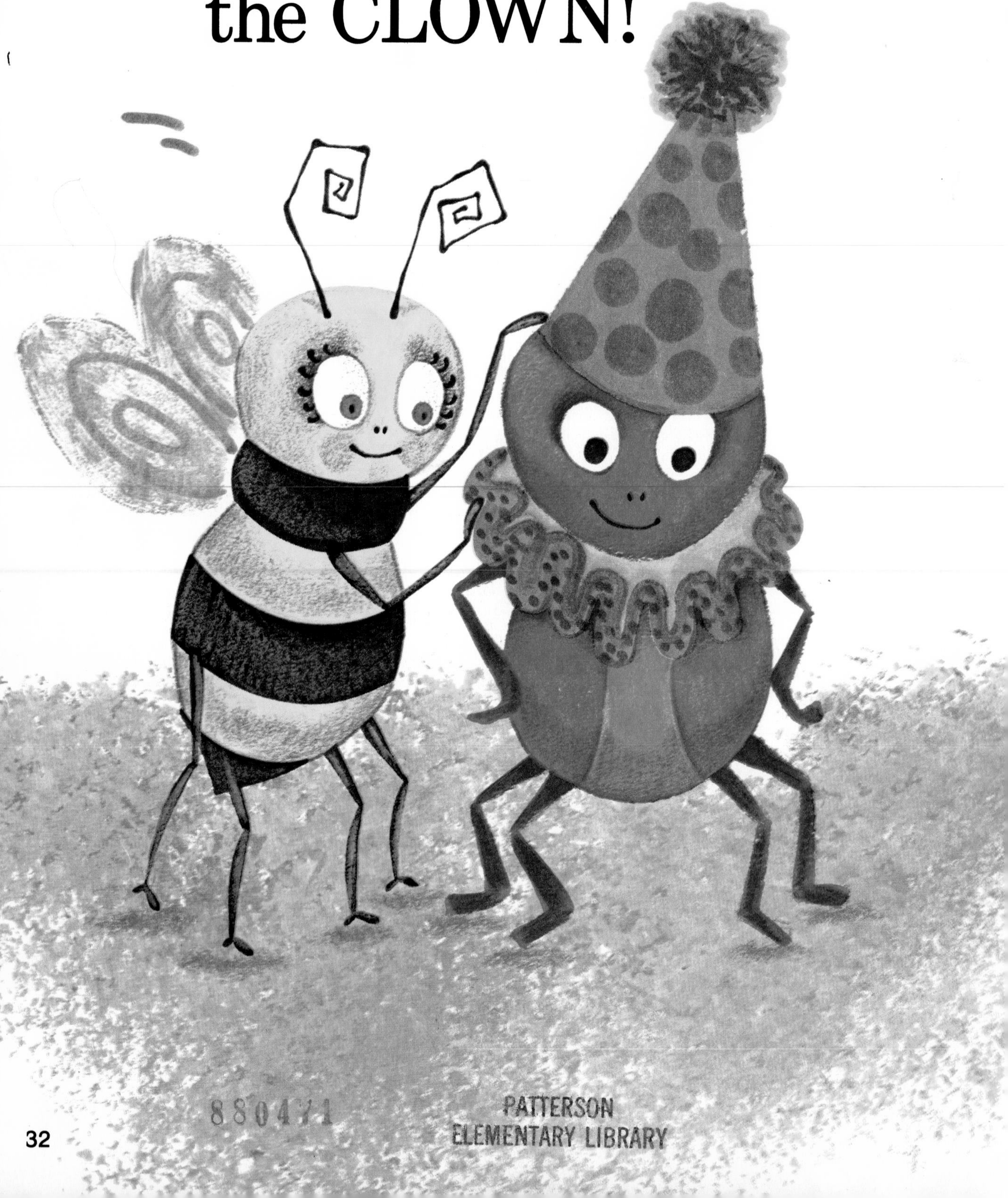